The Clarence

BOOK OF FRIENDS

Jeff ~~(crossed out)~~
Sumo ✩ ✩

AND
OTHER PEOPLE
HE LIKES

BY BRIAN ELLING

CARTOON
NETWORK
B O O K S

AN IMPRINT OF
PENGUIN RANDOM HOUSE

CARTOON NETWORK BOOKS
Penguin Young Readers Group
An Imprint of Penguin Random House LLC

TM and © Cartoon Network. (s16) All rights reserved. Published in 2016 by Cartoon Network Books, an imprint of Penguin Random House LLC, 345 Hudson Street, New York, New York 10014. Manufactured in China.

ISBN 978-0-8431-8342-9   10 9 8 7 6 5 4 3 2 1

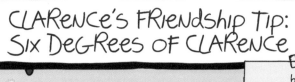

CLARENCE'S FRIENDShip TIP: SIX DeGReeS OF CLARENCE

by Clarence

They SAY you'Re NeveR moRe thAN six people AwAy FROM mAKING A New FRIeNd! ANd it's tRue! FRIeNds WILL pAss Notes to you IN CLAss, sit With you At LuNCh, ANd Let you BoRRow shoRts FOR GyM eveN IF you Get RINGwoRM. But thAt's OKAY. WORMs ARe FRIeNds, too!

 RINGWORM'S NOT SO BAD!

You CAN use the ChARt we mAde oN the Next pAGe to see how CLose you ARe to someoNe you'd WANt to KNow, ANd who you'LL hAve to Go thRouGh to Get some OF thAt sweet FRIeNd time.

 I CONNECTED JEFF TO CLARENCE'S BUTT!

JEFF'S SAMPLE FRIENDSHIP PROFILE & INSTRUCTIONS

by Jeff

OUR ~~MY~~ friendship profiles are designed to measure important metrics and provide statistical data points for the control group in all key demographics.

THERE'S NO "MY" IN the WORD tEAM!

NO *HABLO* SCIENCE!!! I THINK JEFF IS TRYING TO SAY THESE ARE LISTS OF FACTS ABOUT OUR FRIENDS! TO SHOW YOU HOW IT WORKS, CLARENCE AND I FILLED IN THE FAKE FORM ON THE NEXT PAGE.

FRIENDSHIP PROFILE: CLUMO

 IF Sumo And I Got mARRied, this would Be ouR BABy!

BODY: BABy shAped

HAIR: None

MOOD: BuRpy

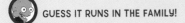 GUESS IT RUNS IN THE FAMILY!

BUDDY STARS: ************

 Good Boy oR GIRL, CLumo! BTW, WhICh ARe you?

PERSONALITY: UNPRedICtABLe

FUTURE JOB: CIRCus LION

 CLumo IS my "pRide" And Joy. Get It?!

LIKES: BABy Food

 I LIKe BABy Food! ThAt must RuN IN the FAMILY, too!

DISLIKES: Bedtime

FAVORITE QUOTE: "MAMA!"

FRIENDS: OtheR BABies.
PICtuRes oF BABies.
BABies oN TV.

SPECIAL TALENTS: DIApeR RAsh

7

FRIENDSHIP PROFILE: CLARENCE

by Sumo

BODY: <u>MEDIUM BIG</u>

HAIR: <u>UNCOMBED</u>

MOOD: <u>HAPPY</u>

BUDDY STARS: ✱✱✱

PERSONALITY: FUN. CLARENCE TREATS EVERY DAY LIKE A NEW ADVENTURE AND ALWAYS MAKES NEW FRIENDS, EVEN IF THEY ARE A BUNCH OF ANGRY RACCOONS. HE GETS IN TROUBLE A LOT, BUT ALWAYS SEES THE BRIGHT SIDE. OH, AND HE ALSO BELIEVES EVERYTHING YOU TELL HIM AND HAS NO IDEA WHAT SARCASM IS!

I WAS IN A SARCASM ONCE. IT WAS REALLY DARK AND HAD BATS LIVING IN IT!

FUTURE JOB: SOME SAY CLARENCE IS A CLASS CLOWN AND THAT HE'LL NEVER AMOUNT TO ANYTHING. BUT HE'LL PROBABLY BE A WORLD-CLASS CELEBRITY. EITHER THAT OR A CLERK AT FOOD NEPHEWS GROCERY STORE FOR THE REST OF HIS LIFE. IT'S A TOSS-UP!

BIGGEST FEAR: SWEATING SO MUCH THAT HE BECOMES A CLARENCE RAISIN

Remember to stay hydrated!

LIKES: FOOD, FRIENDS, GOOD TIMES, GAMES, JOKES, SONGS, FALLING DOWN, HORNS, BOOBY TRAPS, IMAGINARY SMOKE BOMBS, FREE SAMPLES

I ALSO LIKE everything.

DISLIKES: MEAN PEOPLE, READING MAPS

FAVORITE QUOTE: "I SCREWED THIS UP MYSELF. NOW I GOTTA SCREW IT DOWN MYSELF."

FRIENDS: SUMO (BEST FRIEND). JEFF (BEST FRIEND). AMY GILLIS, CHAD, EVERYONE ELSE, WIZARDS, AND ALL ANIMALS (REAL AND IMAGINARY)

SPECIAL TALENTS: PENCIL WALRUS IMPERSONATION, MUD SCULPTING, TAKING JEFF'S FRIES

I've seen Clarence do things to fries that no man should have to see.

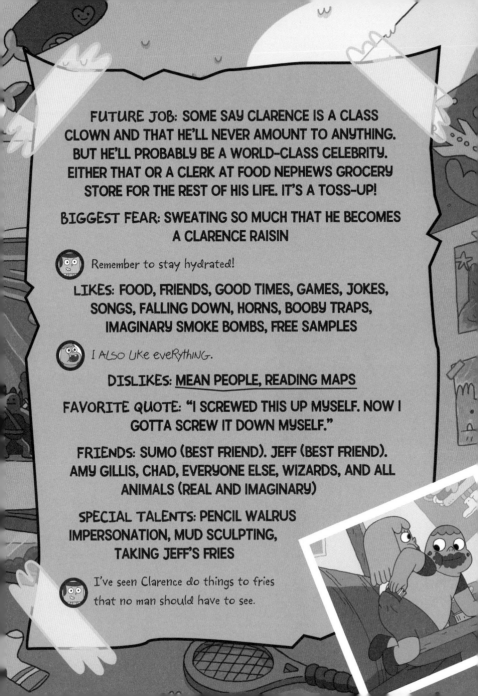

FRIENDSHIP PROFILE:
Sumo ~~AKA RYAN SUMOZSKI~~

by Clarence

DON'T CALL ME RYAN!

BODY: SCRAGGLY

HAIR: Shaved

MOOD: WILD

BUDDY STARS: ★★★★☆

Those don't look like real buddy stars!

CLARENCE DREW THEM. TWO CAN PLAY AT THAT GAME, MS. BAKER!

PERSONALITY: Sumo is a loose cannon. But the kind of cannon that shoots out clowns or something really fun. You never know what he's going to do! He's not afraid of anything, has his own way of being polite, and is really smart, but in a way that teachers don't always appreciate.

10

SECRET FACT: Sumo is the LEAST GULLIBLE person I know, probably because he has older brothers who tell him secrets only teenagers know.

BIGGEST FEAR: Authority Figures (teachers, police, parents)

LIKES: Rabid dogs, drawing on desks, running on all fours, thrift stores, the smell of fear musk, junkyards, making fart sounds instead of using words, free potato chips

DISLIKES: Jeff when he acts like a ~~SNOB~~ gentleman, rules, school, gentlemanly conduct

I think Clarence meant to write the word "gentleman" here. Don't worry, I fixed it.

FAVORITE QUOTE: "We could hunt for roadkill. I found a skunk last week, still had most of its head."

FRIENDS: CLARENCE, JEFF

SPECIAL TALENTS: Punching people who wake him up, boat building, drinking milk from the container

If you want Sumo to like you, but don't know him that well... don't look him in the eye. It makes him uncomfortable.

11

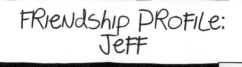

FRIENDSHIP PROFILE: Jeff

by Jeff

THIS GUY NEEDS TO LIGHTEN UP!

BODY: <u>Elegantly thin</u>

HAIR: <u>Square</u>

MOOD: <u>Discerning</u>

BUDDY STARS: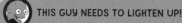

(and counting)

PERSONALITY: Jeff is perfect in every way, no matter what the test scores show. Some people say he has a really hard time having fun, but it's just not true. He simply does things in his own way that only makes sense in his brilliant mind.

AS JEFF'S BEST FRIEND, I UNDERSTAND HIS SPECIAL NEEDS, AND THE IMPORTANCE OF IGNORING THEM.

FUN FACT: Teachers and parents love Jeff.

I WOULDN'T BE FRIENDS WITH ADULTS. THEY'LL TURN ON YOU!

BIGGEST FEAR: <u>Being too perfect</u>

LIKES: Perfect circles, the federal court system, hand sanitizer, a neat closet, sandwiches with the edges cut off, untouched toys in their original packaging

DISLIKES: Scout meals with hamburgers (YUCK!), not having perfect vision, ball pits, head bumps, fist bumps, goose bumps, any type of bumps

FAVORITE QUOTE: "I have my own complex reasons for things. Things you could never understand. Reasons for people to never touch my fries."

FRIENDS: Clarence, Sumo, Ms. Baker, current and former US presidents, his moms

SPECIAL TALENTS: <u>Worrying, showering</u>

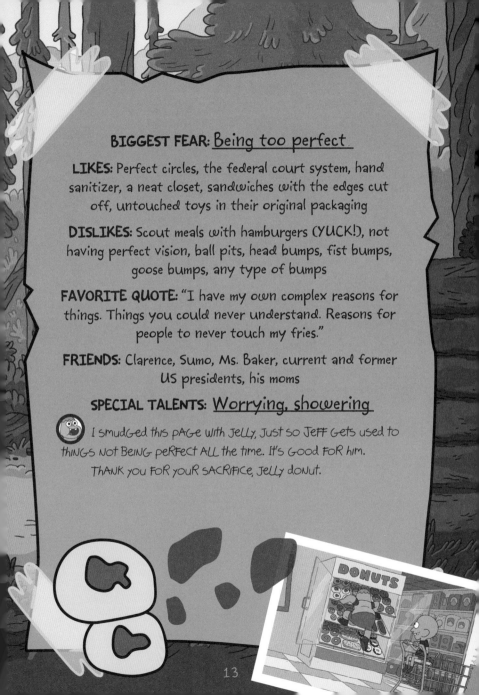 I SMUDGED THIS PAGE WITH JELLY, JUST SO JEFF GETS USED TO THINGS NOT BEING PERFECT ALL THE TIME. IT'S GOOD FOR HIM. THANK YOU FOR YOUR SACRIFICE, JELLY DONUT.

JEFF'S FRIENDSHIP TIP: BEING A GOOD DESK NEIGHBOR

by
Jeff

Being a proper desk neighbor is really important if you want to avoid another complete meltdown of social order, as anyone who remembers the week of "Clarence Dollars" will tell you.

THOSE WERE THE DAYS!

Here are my tips on how to be a good desk neighbor:

1. Keep your arms and legs inside the desk at all times. If you don't, someone who is rushing to be the first to help Ms. Baker may trip.

2. Never, ever change seats! Remember your seat in the classroom and sit there for the entire year! Changing seats will create a domino effect of total panic that could alter the universe as we know it forever!

3. Keep shoes on at all times. Phew! Enough said.

4. Sit up straight in your chair. Don't wiggle around, slouch, or bang your head on the desk. Sit on the chair. Not on the floor. Not on the shoulders of the person behind you. On the chair. That's what chairs are for. Why is this so hard for people?

I LiKe to sit ON my heAd so my FACe KNows whAt it FeeLs LiKe to Be my BACK poCKet!

5. Mouths are to remain closed, unless you've been asked to answer a question! Mouth breathers, this means you! No one wants to feel someone panting on the back of their neck!

TRY SLEEPING IN ONE BEDROOM WITH FIFTEEN OF YOUR BROTHERS AND SISTERS EVERY NIGHT. THERE'S SO MUCH BREATHING GOING ON IN THERE, SOMETIMES I GET BLOWN INTO THE LIVING ROOM.

FRiENDShiP PROFiLE:
Amy (GiLLiS)

by Clarence

BODY: AthLetiC

HAiR: Bike helmet

MOOD: Up FOR ANything

BUDDY STARS: **********

PERSONALiTY: Amy is A ReALLy COOL GiRL Who is BetteR At doiNG Boy stuff thAN most OF the Boys ARe. She Likes spORts ANd RidiNG Bikes ANd CLiMBiNG, ANd isN't AFRAid OF GettiNG diRty. She's ALSO ReALLy BRAve. Not eveN BeLSON CAN iNtimidAte heR! She's pRetty muCh the Best GiRL eveR!

SECRET FACT: Amy ALSO hAS A SOFt Side. Like WheN She tALks ABout the FiRe-BReAthiNG dRAGONS FROM heR FANtAsy Novels.

AMY IS SO STRONG, SHE CAN RIDE HER BIKE UPHILL, EVEN WHILE CLARENCE IS STANDING ON THE PEGS WITH A BACKPACK FULL OF SANDWICHES. FOR THAT SHE DESERVES AN OLYMPIC MEDAL!

BIGGEST FEAR: WheRe she wILL Go to school Next yeAR

LIKES: MAps, LizARd tAiLs, pRetendiNG to Be A BeAR

DISLIKES: CLAReNCe's RAp, BeLsoN, FLyiNG piNeCoNes

I SAW HER TAKE A PINECONE TO THE FACE, AND SHE DIDN'T EVEN FLINCH! NOW, THAT'S AWESOME! IT LOOKED LIKE THIS . . .

FAVORITE QUOTE: "WhAtever. It didN't eveN ReALLy huRt."

FRIENDS: CLAReNCe

SPECIAL TALENTS: KNowiNG whAt AN eRRAtic is

Everyone knows what an erratic is. But in case you don't, it's a rock or boulder that has been moved by glacial action. Here's a photo:

17

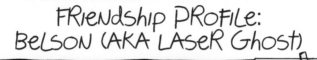

FRiENDShiP PROFile:
BelSON (AKA LASeR Ghost)

by
Jeff

 LASER GHOST! MORE LIKE LASER LOSER!

BODY: <u>Bowling ball</u>

HAIR: <u>Unibrow</u>

MOOD: <u>Negative</u>

BUDDY STARS: ****

PERSONALITY: Belson is less nice than some of the other students in school. That's about all I can say about him without getting into trouble with Ms. Baker.

JEFF'S BEING TOO NICE. BELSON IS A BULLY! BUT HIS ARMS ARE TOO SHORT TO DO ANY REAL BULLY STUFF, SO INSTEAD HE JUST SAYS MEAN STUFF TO HURT PEOPLE'S FEELINGS.

STRANGE FACT: Belson can play video games all day long, even *Hot Dog Police 2*, which is the exact same as *Hot Dog Police 1* (if you ask me).

BIGGEST FEAR: That no one will come to his sleepover

LIKES: Intense video games

18

I KNOW ONE OTHER THING BELSON LIKES, BUT IT'S A SECRET... HE LOVES BABY DOLPHINS. I BET HE'D KISS ONE ON THE BLOWHOLE IF HE COULD.

DISLIKES: People, getting hit in the face with moss, losing at laser tag, zoos (except for Cheetah Town Safari), the buddy system, daytime, nighttime, air, water, earth, colors, sound, bathrooms, bedrooms, all rooms, the outdoors, compliments, sentences, science, school, all things not called school, nouns, verbs, punctuation (especially commas), polite conversation, happiness, songs, butterflies, pancakes, breakfast foods, dinner foods, all foods, continents, weather, gravity, the way the moon changes shape without asking his permission, outer space, molecules, imagination, things that exist, things that will exist or used to exist, time, things that move, things that are still, puzzles, anything not already listed on this list, and lists

FAVORITE QUOTE:
"Why are you still in my house?"

FRIENDS: Nathan, Percy, Dustin, Clarence

FRiENDShiP PROFiLE: BReehn

by Jeff

BODY: <u>Old-timey thermometer</u>

HAIR: <u>Ginger</u>

MOOD: <u>Anxious</u>

BUDDY STARS: **********

PERSONALITY: Breehn is so nervous! Probably because he wants to make sure everything is perfect. Or because his parents renovated their house and now he has to make sure Clarence doesn't wreck it.

OR MAYBE BECAUSE HIS MOM IS SECRETLY A DEMON FROM THE UNDERWORLD (JUST A GUESS).

BIGGEST FEAR: <u>Near-lethal peanut allergy</u>

WHEN BReehn Ate peANut ButteR At the zoo, his FACe BLew up Like A BALLoon. I CAN'T iMAGiNe WhAT iT's Like to Be AttACked By Food! Food is Like oNe oF my Best FRieNds.

0•20

LIKES: Scaring Clarence with a horn, being polite

DISLIKES: Exploding chemistry experiments, upsetting his parents, having Ms. Baker reach down his throat for a peanut-butter sandwich

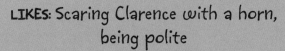 I WISH I COULD HAVE SEEN THIS IN PERSON! BUT I WAS SICK THAT DAY BECAUSE I KEEP SLEEPING OUTDOORS! I GOTTA REMEMBER TO GO INSIDE WHEN IT'S DARK OUT.

FAVORITE QUOTE: "Don't be a good host. Be a great host!"

FRIENDS: Clarence, Jeff, Sumo, Blaide, Chelsea, Percy

SECRET BEST FRIEND: <u>Jeff</u>

BReehN LiKes tAPAS ANd ALWAYS WeARs A Bow tie, WhicH meANs JeFF thiNks he's pRetty much the Next Best thiNg siNce desk ORGANiZeRs.

SPECIAL TALENTS: Playing by the rules

Sumo's Friendship Tip: Are You A Good Friend?

by Sumo

LOYALTY IS IMPORTANT IN GOOD FRIENDSHIPS.

SO ARE LAUGHING AND SLEEPOVERS. TO DECIDE IF YOU ARE A GOOD FRIEND OR NOT, ASK YOURSELF THESE SIMPLE QUESTIONS:

1. IF YOU WERE ON A DESERTED ISLAND WITH YOUR FRIEND AND COULD ONLY LISTEN TO ONE SONG, WOULD YOU LET THIS PERSON LISTEN TO "HAPPY BIRTHDAY TO ME" ON REPEAT FOREVER?

 This seems unlikely to occur, Sumo.

2. WOULD YOU EAT A BUG FOR THAT PERSON?

 ALWAYS, UNLESS THAT BUG WAS MY FRIEND.

3. IF THIS PERSON ASKED TO BORROW YOUR SOCKS AND THEN GAVE THEM BACK, WOULD YOU STILL WEAR THEM?

 Ahhh, no! And no!

4. IF YOUR FRIEND CLOSED THEIR EYES AND FELL BACKWARD, WOULD YOU CATCH THEM?

 It depends on how much they weigh.

5. WOULD YOU TELL THIS PERSON A SECRET YOU KNEW, EVEN THOUGH YOU TOLD SOMEONE ELSE YOU'D NEVER TELL ANYONE?

 Yes, But . . . shhhhh! It's A secRet.

6. IF YOUR FRIEND BROKE THEIR ARM, WOULD YOU WRITE SOMETHING NICE ON THEIR CAST?

7. WOULD YOU SHARE FOOD WITH THIS PERSON IF THEY WERE EATING IT WITH THEIR HANDS OR FEET?

 Is theRe Any otheR WAy to eAt Food?

IF YOU ANSWERED YES TO ANY OF THESE QUESTIONS, CONGRATULATIONS! YOU ARE A GOOD FRIEND!

FRIENDSHIP PROFILE: PERCY

by Clarence

BODY: BABY SNOWMAN

HAIRS: ThReE

MOOD: SensitivE

BUDDY STARS: *************

PERSONALITY: PeRCy is sweet And iNNOCeNt, Like A FLOWeR . . . iF FLOWeRs tRipped ANd FELL DOWN A Lot. He seems YOUNG ANd is eAsiLY AFFeCted By thiNGs ANd WiLL CRy iF he's upset. No mAtteR WHo's WAtChiNG. WhiCh i thiNk shows thAt he's ReALLy BRAve!

SECRET STRUGGLE: PeRCy tRies to Keep up, But No mAtteR WhAt, he ALWAys seems to eNd up iN A uRiNAL.

BIGGEST FEAR: <u>SpideR AttACk to the Nose</u>

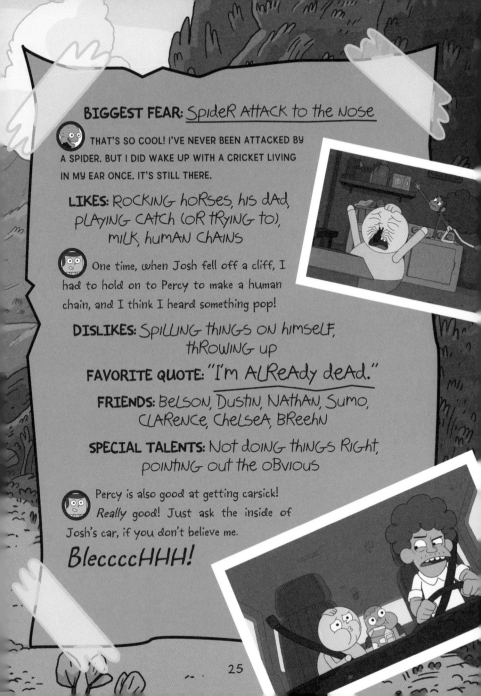

THAT'S SO COOL! I'VE NEVER BEEN ATTACKED BY A SPIDER. BUT I DID WAKE UP WITH A CRICKET LIVING IN MY EAR ONCE. IT'S STILL THERE.

LIKES: ROCKING hoRSeS, his dAd, PLAYING CAtCh (OR tRYING to), mILK, humAN ChAINS

One time, when Josh fell off a cliff, I had to hold on to Percy to make a human chain, and I think I heard something pop!

DISLIKES: SPILLING thINGS ON himseLf, thROWING up

FAVORITE QUOTE: <u>"I'm ALReAdy deAd."</u>

FRIENDS: BeLSON, DustiN, NAthAN, Sumo, CLAReNCe, ChelseA, BReehN

SPECIAL TALENTS: Not doING thINGS RIGht, POINtING out the oBvIous

Percy is also good at getting carsick! *Really* good! Just ask the inside of Josh's car, if you don't believe me.

BleccccHHH!

FRIENDSHIP PROFILE: MALESSICA

by Sumo

BODY: HARD-BOILED EGG

HAIR: NOT WASHED

MOOD: CURIOUS

BUDDY STARS: *************

+ 1 POINT FOR JEFF!

PERSONALITY: MALESSICA'S GOT HUGE GLASSES AND DOES HER HOMEWORK AND IS REALLY SHY ABOUT HER FEELINGS FOR BOYS, ESPECIALLY JEFF. ESPECIALLY SINCE THE ORIGAMI TOLD HER THAT HE MIGHT NOT LIKE HER.

I told you she likes me! YES! Point one for Jeff!

FUTURE JOB: PROFESSIONAL SKYDIVER

SECRET FACT: MALESSICA REALLY CAME OUT OF HER SHELL AT A SLEEPOVER, WHEN CLARENCE GOT HER TO RELEASE HER CRAZY SIDE!

BIGGEST FEAR: THAT HER ORIGAMI LIES TO HER

LIKES: JEFF, SCREAMING IN UNISON, PLAYING DRESS-UP, GLITTER

DISLIKES: JOINING CLARENCE'S "HUG FORCE," BOY HORSES, JEFF

 That ended quick. ☹

FAVORITE QUOTE: "EEEEEEEEEK!"

FRIENDS: KIMBY, COURTLIN, DARLIE, JEFF, CLARENCE

SPECIAL TALENTS: TOILET PAPERING TREES

KNOWING MALESSICA tAUGHT me thAT GIRLS ARe SO FUN . . . AND thAT GIGGLING CAN GO ON FOR hOURS BEFORE you PASS out.

CLARENCE'S FRIENDSHIP TIP:
NEW FRIEND ICEBREAKERS

by
Clarence

WE ALL NEED FRIENDS. AND MORE THAN LIKELY, YOU COULD ALWAYS USE ONE MORE, YOU KNOW, IN CASE OF A FOOD FIGHT OR SOMETHING.

BUT TAKING THAT FIRST STEP CAN BE HARD. HERE'S SOME WAYS TO START A CONVERSATION WITH A NEW BFF.

Hey, WANT TO COME OVER TO MY HOUSE AND BREAK WOOD WITH A HAMMER?

Hello. Would you like to be my new best friend? I'm available starting now if you have some hand sanitizer.

YOU REMIND ME OF SOMEONE WHO WANTS TO GO to the MOVIES WITH ME. DO YOU?

I'VE GOT A TWO-HEADED GRASSHOPPER. WANT TO SEE?

🦫 WoW! It Looks LiKe my pARents FoRGot to pick me up, too. RoAd tRip!

🦫 OH, HEY! LOOKS LIKE YOU DROPPED YOUR ALL-ACCESS PASS TO MY BACKYARD. BAM!

🦫 YoU LooK LoneLy. WAnt to CHAnGe thAt?

🦫 I noticed you were sitting alone. May I join you and then tell you all my deepest secrets?

🦫 Pssst! I've Got A piÑAtA FuLL oF Bees. InteRested?

🦫 HOWDY, STRANGER! LET'S MAKE THIS THE LAST TIME I SAY THAT TO YOU.

🦫 WouLd you LiKe to CReAte A seCRet hAndshAke with me?

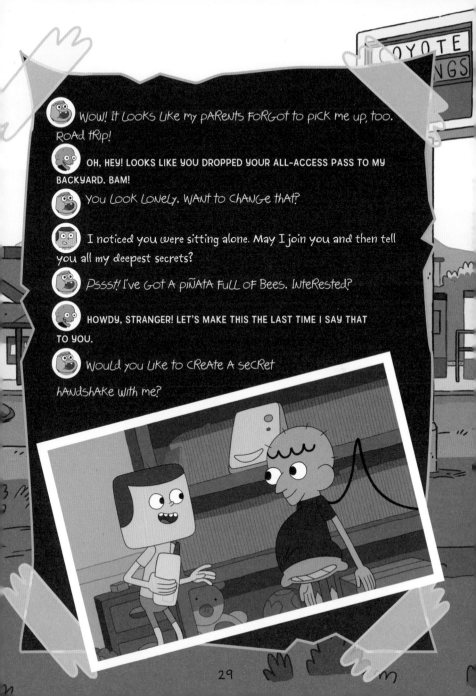

29

FRIENDShip PROFILE:
Ashley

by
Clarence

BODY: <u>LOLLIPOP</u>
HAIR: <u>PONYtAIL</u>
MOOD: <u>CONFIDENT</u>
BUDDY STARS: *******
AND A 1/2

PERSONALITY: AshLey LIkes to tAKE CHANCes. Not ONLy did she Let my toy motORCyCLe do A BACKFLIP oveR heR BINdeR, she ALSo ASKed me to Be heR BoyFRIeNd ANd theN ACTuALLy showed up to the dAte. ALONe. THAt IS SO Awesome!

 WATCH OUT, ABERDALE! CLARENCE SNAGGED A GIRLFRIEND!

Just for the record, Clarence and Ashley broke up after only one date. And it didn't go well.

SECRET PASSION: AshLey's pRetty mAtuRe ANd Goes oN dAtes to RestAuRANts, But stILL hASN't Lost heR FuN side. She stILL LIKes to pLAy IN the mud.

BIGGEST FEAR: GettING CAuGht ON A deseRted ISLANd WItH NO FLARes.

30

MY BROTHER'S GOT, LIKE, THREE GIRLFRIENDS, AND BIG SHOULDERS. THAT'S HOW I KNEW THAT ASHLEY WOULD LIKE CLARENCE MORE IF HE WORE SHOULDER PADS!

LIKES: School BiNDeRs, ChOcOLAte miLKShAKes, AwKwARd pAuses, FRogs

DISLIKES: Getting A ChOcOLAte miLKShaKe spiLLeD oN heR

FAVORITE QUOTE: "So, I Guess we'Re supposed to Go oN A dAte NOw?"

FRIENDS: ChelseA, ALisoN, Amy, CLAReNCe

SPECIAL TALENTS: DiNNeR CoNveRsAtion, mAKiNG the FiRst move

31

FRIENDSHIP PROFILE: BRADY

by
Jeff

BODY: <u>Regular type</u>

HAIR: <u>Blond</u>

MOOD: <u>Doubtful</u>

BUDDY STARS: ********

PERSONALITY: Brady is shy most of the time. He always thinks he's not good enough and is afraid to talk to people, so instead he talks to himself in his own head.

SOMETIMES I HEAR VOICES IN MY HEAD, TOO. MOSTLY I IGNORE THEM, BUT SOMETIMES THEY MAKE ME DO STUFF. FUN STUFF.

STRANGE FACT: Clarence thinks Brady's name is Harvely.

Oh NO! THIS ISN'T HARVELY. Oh, CHICKEN NUGGETS! I messed UP AGAIN. WHO'S HARVELY, THEN? AM I HARVELY? WHAT IF I'VE BEEN HARVELY THIS WHOLE TIME?

32

BIGGEST FEAR: Not being able to make a decision

LIKES: Girls with red hair, inner monologues, the fetal position, the Grand Canyon

DISLIKES: Names that start with the number 2, road trips without a car, eating spaghetti like dogs in the movies, leeches, Clarence in his underwear while wearing an apron

FAVORITE QUOTE:
"She doesn't even know I exist."

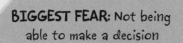 NOW *THERE'S* A QUOTE JEFF CAN RELATE TO!

FRIENDS: Clarence

SPECIAL TALENTS: Running from hoboes, lifesaving decision making, understanding the Aberdale bus system

I OWE HARVEY MY LIFE. IF IT WASN'T FOR HIM, I WOULD HAVE USED THAT FISHING ROD TO TRY TO REEL IN A SPEEDING TRUCK, AND I WOULDN'T HAVE HAD THE BEST TIME EVER.

FRIENDSHIP PROFILE: Emilio

by Sumo

BODY: <u>MOSTLY JUST A HEAD</u>

HAIR: <u>LIKE ELVIS, BUT BETTER</u>

MOOD: <u>BRAVE (SORT OF)</u>

BUDDY STARS: ********

PERSONALITY: EMILIO LIKES TO ACT TOUGH, BUT DEEP INSIDE, HE GETS SCARED LIKE EVERYONE ELSE. HE'S ALWAYS GOT A WITTY COMMENT TO SAY AND IS THE LEADER OF HIS FRIENDS, JULIEN AND MEMO.

SCARY FACT: EMILIO IS FUN BUT CAN COME ACROSS TOO HARSH SOMETIMES, LIKE WHEN HE SAID THAT HE WOULDN'T MIND IF BELSON GOT KIDNAPPED BY A SERIAL KILLER (I MEAN, WE ALL THINK IT, BUT WE DON'T SAY IT OUT LOUD).

BIGGEST FEAR: NOT BEING GOOD AT PLAYING *PSYCHOPATHIC ICE-CREAM MAN*

34

I thought it would have been chain saws. Interesting.

LIKES: SLEEPING BAGS, RC CARS

DISLIKES: <u>SCARY STORIES</u>

FAVORITE QUOTE: "HE PUT TOOTHPASTE ON HIS CHONIES."

What are chonies? I hope I don't have any!

FRIENDS: MEMO, JULIEN, JEFF, SUMO, DUSTIN, CLARENCE

SPECIAL TALENTS: SCREAMING WHEN NO ONE ELSE DOES

AGHGGHAHAHA!

SORRY. COULDN'T help myself.

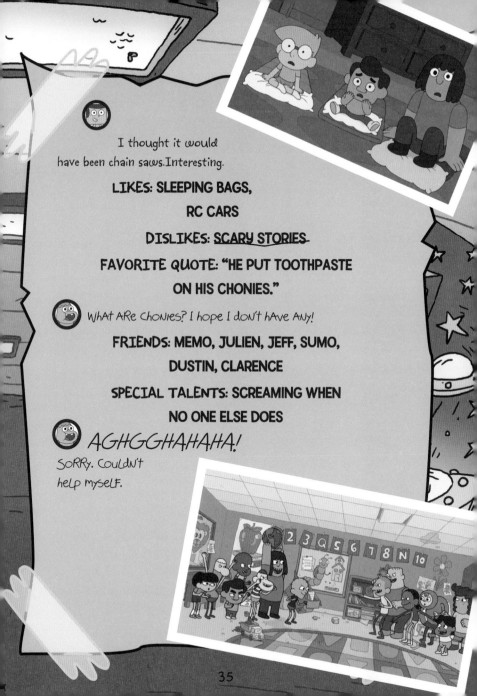

Sumo's FRiENdShip Tip: The ARt oF CoNVeRSAtioN

by Sumo

MAKING FRIENDS REQUIRES GOOD CONVERSATION SKILLS.

TO KEEP YOUR FRIENDS ENTERTAINED, TELL A STORY LIKE THESE ONES:

I RemembeR the time I put thAt toy BetweeN my teeth And then AshLey Asked me to Be heR BoyFRieNd. And I swALLowed it. And Now it's pARt of my LuNG.

ONCE I PLAYED A VIDEO GAME AT THE PIZZA SWAMP UNTIL THE CONTROLLERS BROKE OFF IN MY HANDS. I DON'T KNOW IF THAT MEANS I WON OR NOT.

I know the history of the protractor. It all started in 1653.

ONe time, ChAd ANd I weRe wAtchiNG TV, ANd we stAyed theRe FoR FouR dAys without eveN eAtiNG. And theN wheN I did eAt, my stomAch wAs so smALL, I Felt FuLL AFteR oNe FReNch FRy.

IF THAT DOESN'T WORK, REMEMBER YOU CAN ALWAYS TELL JOKES.
JUST MAKE SURE THEY'RE FUNNY, LIKE THESE CLASSICS!

 A toASteR WALKed iNto A RestAuRANt ANd ASKed FoR A
dRiNK. The WAiteR SAid, "SORRy, We'Re CLosed." ANd the toASteR
SAid, "Oh, CRumBS!"

What's the difference between a piano and a fish? You can't
tuna fish!

WHAT DID THE FOREST SAY WHEN SOMEONE STOLE ITS BATHING SUIT?
"OH NO! WHO TOOK MY TREE TRUNKS?"

FRIENDSHIP PROFILE:
MALAKEVIN

by
Sumo

 I think "Malakevin" is Hawaiian for "bonkers."

 ALOHA, MALAKEVIN!

BODY: <u>SAUSAGE</u>

HAIR: <u>MESSY</u>

MOOD: <u>CRAZY</u>

BUDDY STARS: <u>UNKNOWN</u>

PERSONALITY: THERE'S SOMETHING OFF ABOUT MALAKEVIN. HE'S SUPER SERIOUS AND INTENSE. NOT ONLY THAT, HE'S ALWAYS SAYING WEIRD STUFF THAT NO ONE UNDERSTANDS.

STRANGE FACT: MALAKEVIN CHEWED ON JEFF'S LEG ONE TIME.

BIGGEST FEAR: GETTING HIT WITH A LEAF BLOWER

 DANGER! DANGER!

LIKES: READING HIS PARENTS' HISTORY BOOKS, GRASSY KNOLLS, EATING MONEY

DISLIKES: GETTING HIS ARM CAUGHT IN A STORM DRAIN

FAVORITE QUOTE: "LIFE IS BUT A DANCE OF TRIUMPH AND TRAGEDY."

FRIENDS: CLARENCE

SPECIAL TALENTS: FINDING DOLLARS, ATTEMPTED CANNIBALISM

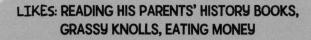 I ALWAYS MEANT TO ASK MALAKEVIN WHAT JEFF TASTED LIKE. PROBABLY A SUPERFOOD, LIKE BLUEBERRIES!

FRieNdSHip PROFiLe: ChelseA

by Sumo

BODY: <u>TALL</u>

HAIR: <u>GIGANTIC</u>

MOOD: <u>UNEXPECTED</u>

BUDDY STARS: ********

PERSONALITY: ON THE OUTSIDE, CHELSEA LOOKS REALLY INNOCENT. BUT DON'T BE FOOLED! BEHIND THOSE SHINY BRACES LIES A WILD SPIRIT JUST WAITING TO BE UNLEASHED THE MOMENT SHE IS LEFT ALONE AT A DINNER PARTY.

 ONCE I SAW heR KNOCK JeFF doWN USING ONLy heR hAIR! ThAT WAS AWesome!

FUN FACT: ONCE CHELSEA GETS GOING, THERE'S NO TELLING WHAT SHE CAN DO. YOU MIGHT EVEN FIND HER WITH ROLLER SKATES ON HER HANDS! UNBELIEVABLE!

BIGGEST FEAR:

<u>NOT TAKING A DARE</u>

40

LIKES: DANGER, SPILLING NAILS ON THE FLOOR, HANGING WITH BOYS, SCARY ATTICS, CREEPY BASEMENTS, WINNING AT *MONEY BROOM*

DISLIKES: <u>WIMPS, REGRETS</u>

FAVORITE QUOTE: <u>"OR A DEAD BODY!"</u>

 I think you're supposed to report that to the police.

FRIENDS: ALISON, JEFF, CLARENCE, BREEHN, PERCY, SUMO

SPECIAL TALENTS: RIDING IN A BOX THAT'S BEING DRAGGED BEHIND A VACUUM THAT'S SUCKED ONTO CHAD'S BUTT

YOU KNOW WHAT WAS ROMANTIC? WHEN SUMO AND CHELSEA KISSED. THEY'RE IN LOVE!

WE ARE NOT! WE WERE TRYING TO GROSS EVERYBODY OUT! IT WORKED, DIDN'T IT?!

FUTURE HOME: <u>ARMY TENT</u>

FRIENDSHIP PROFILE: Kimby

by Clarence

BODY: TINY

HAIR: YES, PLEASE (AND WITH A PRETTY BOW)

MOOD: DARING

BUDDY STARS: ******

PERSONALITY: Kimby is A veRy GiRLie GiRL who Loves to hAve sLumBeR pArties. She's veRy shy ARound Boys And would RAtheR GIGGLe with heR fRiends iN heR Room thAN ActuALLy tALk to them. But she LeARNs to Be moRe AdveNtuRous iF you Give heR A chANce to RuN ARound the NeighBoRhood At NiGHt.

SECRET FACT: She eveN smAshed A LAWN GNome! YOu GO, GiRLie GiRL!

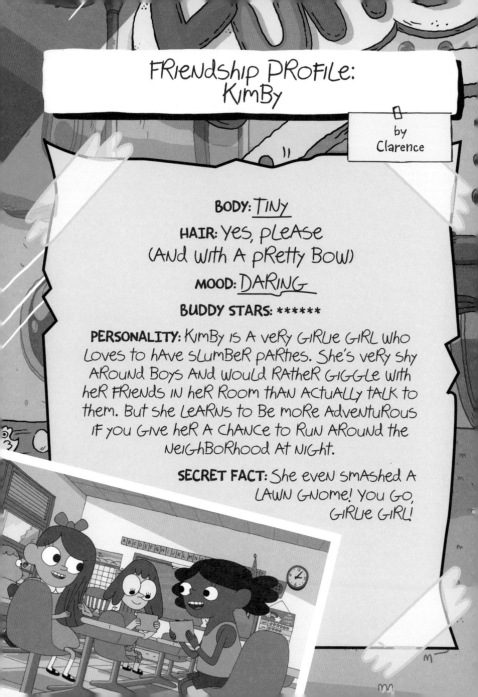

THAT DUDE DIDN'T GNOME WHAT HIT HIM!

BIGGEST FEAR: Split ends

Kimby is always touching her hair. It's a nervous thing. I'm glad I don't do anything like that!

LIKES: Cute ANIMALS, dUCKS, heR hAIR, WeARING fAIRY WINGS

DISLIKES: 20/20 VISION Bees

FAVORITE QUOTE:
"I doN't WANt to touCh youR hAIR."

FRIENDS: MALeSSICA ANd COURtLIN. ANd CLAReNCe!

SPECIAL TALENTS: TAp dANCING WhiLe tiGhtRope WALKING

KIMBY AND I HAVE THE SAME SPECIAL TALENT! WHAT A COINCIDENCE!

JEFF'S FRIENDSHIP TIP:
FRIENDSHIP STUDY BREAK

by
Jeff

Wow. We've done a lot of work (or at least I have).
Time to give our minds a break!

Exercising with friends is a great way to stay motivated.
So grab a friend and dance to the latest song from Kids
to Dudes!

I taught Sumo how to do all their moves!

 I TAUGHT JEFF EVERYTHING HE KNOWS.

Or pretend you're rock stars!

 MAKEUP HELPS TO GET US IN THE MOOD!

Of course, you can always do exercises like push-ups, sit-ups, or jumping jacks.

I thought this WAS supposed to BE A BREAK!

Or, if you're Sumo, run around in circles like a dog who hasn't been out of the house in four days!

IT WAS SIX DAYS. GET IT RIGHT!

FRIENDShip PROFILE: COURTLIN

by Jeff

BODY: Petite   **HAIR:** Pigtails

MOOD: Driven   **BUDDY STARS:** ✶✶✶✶✶✶✶✶

PERSONALITY: Courtlin is tougher than she looks. She stands up for herself and even tells Clarence he's ruining Kimby's slumber party when the other girls are too afraid to say anything! But she'll also go along with the group when it's too fun not to.

STRANGE FACT: Watch out for Courtlin if there's money around . . . Clarence Dollars! She's crazy for them.

LIKES: Sleepovers, boy bands, *Werewolf Boyfriend III*, pajamas

SOMEONE THOUGHT MY DAD WAS A WEREWOLF ONCE. AND HE'S GOT THE SCARS TO PROVE IT.

DISLIKES: Horns (see below)

FAVORITE QUOTE: "Clarence, the horn is, like, super unbecoming on you."

FRIENDS: Kimby, Malessica, Clarence

SPECIAL TALENTS: Performing doll weddings

FRIENDSHIP PROFILE: GILBEN

by Sumo

BODY: <u>STIFF</u>   **HAIR:** <u>DIRTY BEIGE</u>

MOOD: <u>ZONED OUT</u>

BUDDY STARS: NONE (HE ATE THEM)

PERSONALITY: GILBEN IS A MAN OF FEW WORDS. OR NONE, ACTUALLY. HE'S VERY ODD AND USUALLY JUST STARES INTO SPACE, SO IT'S HARD TO TELL WHAT HE'S THINKING. OR IF HE'S THINKING.

STRANGE FACT: GILBEN IS ALWAYS STILL, EVEN WHEN HE'S BEING CARRIED AROUND WHILE HOLDING A BALL IN HIS HANDS AT RECESS.

LIGHT AS A BOARD, STIFF AS A GILBEN. THAT'S WHAT I ALWAYS SAY.

DISLIKES: <u>BLINKING</u>

SPECIAL TALENTS: FALLING OVER WITHOUT MOVING A MUSCLE

Reminder to myself: Do more research on Gilben. Fascinating.

FRIENDSHIP PROFILE: JULIEN

by Clarence

BODY: TALLER THAN SUMO, BUT SHORTER THAN NATHAN

HAIR: MAJORLY BUZZED   **MOOD:** MAJORLY COOL

BUDDY STARS: *****

PERSONALITY: JULIEN DOESN'T LIKE BEING SCARED. HE'D MUCH RATHER JUST WATCH MOVIES AND EAT S'MORES.

FUTURE JOB: FRENCH CHEF

FRIEND FACT: JULIEN HANGS AROUND WITH EMILIO AND MEMO, AND KEEPS OUT OF THE HALLWAYS AS MUCH AS HE CAN. HE'S HARD TO FIND.

I WONDER IF HE'S RELATED TO JULIENNE CARROTS? SHE'S FRENCH.

LIKES: CHEESECAKE PUFFS FOR DINNER

DISLIKES: BEING SCARED A MILLION TIMES FOR NO REASON

FAVORITE QUOTE: "I'M FREAKIN' OUT RIGHT NOW."

FRIENDS: MEMO, EMILIO, NATHAN, CLARENCE

FRiENDShip PROFiLE: NAThAN

by Jeff

BODY: Garbage can   **HAIR:** Bangs only

MOOD: Hard on himself   **BUDDY STARS:** *****

PERSONALITY: Nathan is one of the biggest students in class! He says that he's not very smart, which might be why he doesn't do that great on tests, even though he studies for them. Nathan's got to learn positive thinking!

SECRET FACT: Nathan is a talented artist who likes to draw and read his favorite mystery books, The Henry Boys.

BIGGEST FEAR: Never learning what "making out" means

 MY OLDER BROTHER TOLD ME WHAT MAKING OUT MEANS. BUT I FORGOT BECAUSE IT SOUNDS BORING!

LIKES: Hitting stuff, drawing Clarence Dollars, teasing Belson, girls with soft hair

FAVORITE QUOTE: "I probably won't win."

FRIENDS: Belson, Dustin, Percy, Sumo, Clarence

SPECIAL TALENTS: Looking intimidating, razor-sharp buckteeth

49

FRieNdShip PROFiLe: DuStiN

by Sumo

BODY: <u>CHIMPANZEE</u>

HAIR: <u>ORANGE</u>

MOOD: <u>GO WITH THE FLOW</u>

BUDDY STARS: ****

I GAve DuStiN A CLAReNce DOLLAR FOR GOiNG to the BAthRoom. SometimeS you hAve to RewARd the Little Achievements ANd the BiG oNes! I'm Not suRe which oNe it WAS (I didN't LOOK).

PERSONALITY: DUSTIN IS A FOLLOWER. HE DOES WHATEVER BELSON DOES, BUT IN A MUCH NICER WAY. HE LIKES TO HANG OUT WITH NATHAN AND TALK ABOUT GIRLS, BUT IT'S NOT CLEAR HOW MUCH EITHER OF THEM ACTUALLY KNOW ABOUT WOMEN.

FUTURE JOB: <u>PART-TIME HIP-HOP DANCER</u>

DISLIKES: <u>GOOD POSTURE</u>

FRIENDS: <u>BELSON, NATHAN, PERCY, CLARENCE</u>

SPECIAL TALENTS: RUNNING FAST, DODGEBALL, CAT IMPERSONATIONS

CLARENCE's FRIENDSHIP TIP:
Step Out Of YOUR ComFORt ZONE

by
Clarence

 AND INTO THE CLARENCE ZONE!

JEFF SAYS I MAKE FRIENDS BETTER THAN ANYONE HE KNOWS. SO I'VE WRITTEN MY TIPS ON HOW TO MEET NEW FRIENDS FASTER THAN YOU CAN SAY "IT WAS WORTH IT."

1. TALK TO ANYTHING THAT BREATHES! AND TO SOME THINGS THAT DON'T.

2. REMEMBER NOBODY'S PERFECT. ACCEPTING A NEW FRIEND MEANS ACCEPTING THAT ONE DAY THEY'LL PROBABLY COUGH IN YOUR MOUTH.

 For the record, I disagree with that statement!

3. MEET YOUR NEW FRIEND ON THEIR OWN TURF! EVEN IF THAT MEANS ROLLING AROUND IN A DIRTY BASEMENT!

4. DON'T UNDERESTIMATE THE POWER OF A HUG FORCE!

5. HAVE FUNNN!
   PEOPLE WANT TO TALK TO PEOPLE WHO ARE HAVING FUN.

FRIENDShip PROFILE: BLAIde

by Jeff

BODY: Walking coatrack   **HAIR:** Flat

MOOD: Spastic

BUDDY STARS: *******

PERSONALITY: Blaide might be from another country. He also has an interesting way of holding his hands. But other than that, he's harmless.

BIGGEST FEAR: Missing his bus

LIKES: Porcelain frogs, potted plants, digging with his hands

DISLIKES: Dollar hunts, finding a twenty-dollar bill and then having it swiped out of his hands

FRIENDS: Clarence (sort of)

SPECIAL TALENTS: Covering his ears while Clarence blows an air horn

 Oh, I RemembeR BLAIde NOW!

FRiendship PROFile: GuyleR

by Sumo

BODY: <u>ALL NECK</u>   **HAIR:** <u>SMALL</u>

MOOD: <u>CHILL</u>

BUDDY STARS: *********

PERSONALITY: GUYLER DOESN'T TALK TO ANYBODY. HE'S EITHER REALLY THOUGHTFUL OR A TOTAL PSYCHO. HARD TO TELL.

BIGGEST FEAR: <u>ANYONE SEEING HIS MOUTH</u>

LIKES: FINGER HANDCUFFS, PLAYING THE HORN, TURTLENECKS, CLARENCE DOLLARS

DISLIKES: <u>GETTING REPEATEDLY PUNCHED BY GIRLS</u>

FAVORITE QUOTE: "MMMRRMM. MRRMMR. MMMM."

 HA-HA! THAT WAS A FUNNY JOKE, GUYLER. WHAT DID HE SAY?

FRIENDS: <u>SUMO, CLARENCE</u>

SPECIAL TALENTS: BLINKING, SITTING IN THE BACK ROW OF CLASS

FRIENDShip PROFILE: DARLie

by Jeff

BODY: Tree stump   ~~ICE-CREAM CONE~~
HAIR: ~~Nice~~ ICE-CREAM CONE

MOOD: Peppy   **BUDDY STARS:** ********

 HA! HER HEAD LOOKS LIKE AN ICE-CREAM CONE!

PERSONALITY: Darlie is one of the sweetest girls in school. She likes to giggle and chase people on the playground, but in that way where you know she's just playing and not out to zorch you or something.

BIGGEST FEAR: Loud noises, especially from horns

 YOU MEAN LIKE THIS? *HONK!*

LIKES: The Pledge of Allegiance, Lester's Disease raffles, sweatshirts with huge zipper pulls

DISLIKES: Not being able to hear who won the Lester's Disease raffle

FAVORITE QUOTE: "I heard the math quiz got canceled. Good thing, too. I didn't study much."

FRIENDS: Clarence

54

FRiendship PROFILE: CRendLe

by Clarence

BODY: LOWERCASE LETTER B

HAIR: SLIDING OFF HIS HEAD

MOOD: DREAmy   **BUDDY STARS:** ******************

PERSONALITY: CRENDLE IS EMOTIONAL. EVEN MORE THAN PERCY, WHICH IS HARD TO DO. HE CAN OFTEN BE FOUND STARING INTO SPACE IN A DAZE.

 I KNOW IT WOULD BE ILLEGAL, BUT I'D LIKE TO PUT CRENDLE AND PERCY IN A PIT FIGHT AND SEE WHO WINS!

BIGGEST FEAR: EveRything

LIKES: ThumB-SUCKING, ROCKS, GOOFY SAYINGS, ShoveL pole vAuLts, moNey

FAVORITE QUOTE: "WheRe my mom?"

FRIENDS: Memo, DeBBie, CLARENCE

SPECIAL TALENTS: WALKING IN BALL PITS

 My Clarence Dollars are on Crendle! I heard he hit a trash can at the zoo!

Wham!

FRIEND PROFILE: MAVIS

by Sumo

BODY: <u>MARSHMALLOW</u>   **HAIR:** <u>RED</u>

MOOD: <u>FRIED</u>   **BUDDY STARS:** ✶✶

PERSONALITY: MAVIS DOESN'T TALK TO A LOT OF PEOPLE AT SCHOOL, PROBABLY BECAUSE SHE'S ALWAYS SPENDING TIME WITH THAT FIRE HYDRANT. SHE'S GOT A NERVOUS PERSONALITY THAT MAKES HER VIBRATE WHEN YOU TALK TO HER, WHICH IS "UNIQUE."

BIGGEST FEAR: POORLY MAINTAINED FIRE-SAFETY EQUIPMENT

LIKES: <u>DRINKING HYDRANT WATER</u>

DISLIKES: <u>JUNGLE GYMS, INTERACTION WITH OTHERS</u>

FAVORITE QUOTE: "<u>HURRGHRR?</u>"

FRIENDS: <u>CLARENCE, BRADY (ROMANTIC?)</u>

SPECIAL TALENTS: DANCING IN PLACE WHILE MUMBLING, BLUSHING

This girl is wild! Do you know how many germs are in hydrant water?

FRIENDSHIP PROFILE: ALISON

by Jeff

BODY: Stick figure   **HAIR:** Maroon

MOOD: Dangerous   **BUDDY STARS:** *****

PERSONALITY: Alison is a perky girl who likes to hang out with Chelsea. She can get bored easily at school. When that happens, she's always happy to let her hair down and start a riot! Watch out!

 KICK UP YOUR HEELS, COWGIRL! YEE-HAW!

LIKES: Chelsea's binder, digging in the trash, throwing paper at Ms. Baker

 YOU SHOULD SEE ALISON WRESTLE OVER CLARENCE DOLLARS! SHE'S A MACHINE!

FAVORITE QUOTE:
"No, you are!"

FRIENDS: Chelsea, Clarence

SPECIAL TALENTS: Dumpster diving

FRIENDShip PROFiLE: DeBBie

by Clarence

BODY: CORN-COB hOLDER

HAIR: SO BLOND!

MOOD: FLEXIBLE

BUDDY STARS: ****

PERSONALITY: DeBBie JUST WANTS to BE LiKE everyONe eLSe. She'LL ALWAYS pARTiCiPAtE iN WhAteveR eveRyONe eLSe WANTS to DO. IF iT's popuLAR, DeBBie WiLL MAKE iT even moRe popuLAR!

LIKES: TRENDS

DISLIKES: ALBiNO tiGERS AFTER LABOR DAY

FAVORITE QUOTE: "AGGhGGhGhGhhh!"

FRIENDS: ChELSEA, AShLEY, CLAReNCe

SPECIAL TALENTS: BLENDiNG iNTO A CROWD

JEFF'S FRIENDSHIP TIP: PUTTING YOUR BEST INTO BEING BEST FRIENDS

by Jeff

Being "besties" with Clarence and Sumo is a big commitment. To make sure you keep from letting down your best friends, follow my simple guide:

B—Be the awesomest you can (which is pretty awesome, if you're like me).

E—Exaggerate your best friend's good traits and try to ignore the bad ones, even if there are a lot of them.

S—Supply your friends with healthy snacks.

T—Tell your best friends how much you like them, but not in a mushy way that will make them want to hug you.

I—Include your best friends in all fun activities, like trips to the museum and putting away groceries.

E—Educate your best friends by constantly telling them all the stuff you know.

S—Stand up for your best friends, even if they're wrong.

59

FRIENDShip PROFiLE: SAMUEL

by Clarence

BODY: ORB   **HAIR:** CURLy

MOOD: EASy-pEASy   **BUDDY STARS:** *******

PERSONALITY: SAMUEL IS SO NICE. He COULDN'T hARM A FLY, EVEN IF ThAT FLY WAS tRYING TO ROB him.

Samuel actually seems cool. I might make friends with him, unless that fly landed on him. If it did, it's over.

FRIENDship PROFiLE: PATSiE

by Jeff

BODY: Tiny   **HAIR:** Curly yellow

MOOD: Too comfortable   **BUDDY STARS:** *******

PERSONALITY: Patsie hasn't lost some of those bad habits that most other students stopped doing three years ago, at least in public (see Special Talents to see what I mean).

SPECIAL TALENTS: Nose picking

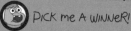

PiCK ME A WINNER!

FRiendship PROFiLe:
TRY

by Sumo

BODY: <u>HUGE</u> HAIR: <u>TALLER ON ONE SIDE</u>

MOOD: <u>DISAPPOINTED</u>   BUDDY STARS: ****

PERSONALITY: LIKE THE BLUE WHALE,
TRY IS A GENTLE GIANT.

FAVORITE QUOTE: "BUT THE CLAW
KEEPS DROPPING IT."

We BoNDed At the PizzA SWAmp. It WAS GReAt!

FRiendship PROFiLe:
MARLie

by Sumo

BODY: <u>ROUND</u>   HAIR: DIRTY BLOND

MOOD: <u>SWEET</u>   BUDDY STARS: ****

PERSONALITY: MARLIE LOVES ALL KINDS OF
SOFT FRILLY THINGS.

WheNeVeR MARLie SmiLeS,
A teddy BeAR Gets its WiNGS!

FRIENDSHIP PROFILE: Memo

by Jeff

BODY: <u>Biggish</u>   **HAIR:** <u>Bushy</u>

MOOD: <u>Stony</u>   **BUDDY STARS:** ***

PERSONALITY: Memo is best friends with Emilio, who needs Memo's muscle to make him look tough. In return, Memo doesn't have to talk. It's a win-win!

DISLIKES: <u>Practical jokes on his chonies.</u>

 Memo is one of my best chonies! Did I use that word right?

FRIENDSHIP PROFILE: Kennan

by Jeff

BODY: <u>Hunchback</u>   **HAIR:** <u>Bangs</u>

MOOD: <u>Bouncy</u>   **BUDDY STARS:** ***

PERSONALITY: Kennan likes to keep himself away from the rest of the group.

I think this guy's got potential ... for ringing bells in a tower or something! That's cool.

FRIENDSHIP PROFILE:
Sumo's BROTHERS AND SISTERS

by
Clarence

BODY: VARIOUS   **HAIR:** FULL OF LICE

MOOD: ENERGETIC   **BUDDY STARS:** 0

MY BROTHERS AND SISTERS MEAN EVERYTHING TO ME! ALL TWELVE OF THEM. OR IS IT FOURTEEN?

PERSONALITY: Sumo's BROTHERS AND SISTERS ARE A LOT LIKE A BUNCH OF WOLVES. They move IN PACKS, AND SOME OF THEM MIGHT HAVE RABIES.

BIGGEST FEAR: NONE

LIKES: CHASING AFTER GINSBOTS, SLEEPING, EATING, SNORING

DISLIKES: BATHING, WEARING CLOTHES

FAVORITE QUOTE: "I'M GONNA BREAK YOU!"

FRIENDS: EACH OTHER, BUGS

SPECIAL TALENTS: CHASING. RUNNING. SCREAMING.

I can't tell them apart! Can you?

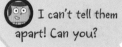

JEFF'S FRIENDSHIP TIP:
Adults . . . FRIENDS OR OH NO?

by
Jeff

Not everyone considers it possible, but adults can
be our friends, too. Why not? I've had some of my best
conversations with adults.

 DON'T DO IT. THEY'LL TURN ON YOU!

Just the other night, Belson's mom and I had a wonderful
conversation. We laughed until the dishes were done! Here
are some special reasons that adults are good
friends to have:

1. Adults can drive us places.

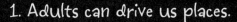 SuRe BeAtS WALKING. IF they RememBeR to pICK you up. ☺

2. Adults have money to
pay for things.

THAT'S WHAT THEY WANT YOU TO THINK!

3. Adults know stuff we don't know.

THEY CAN'T BE TRUSTED!

4. Adults want what's best for us.

5. Adults make food that
we need to live.

Mmmmmm! EGG SALAd!

FRIENDSHIP PROFILE: MS. BAKER

by Jeff

BODY: Tense in the shoulders

HAIR: Long and flowing

MOOD: Airy

BUDDY STARS: As many as she wants

PERSONALITY: Ms. Baker is an amazing teacher. And she's smart. She wears glasses and knows all the planets. She can get overwhelmed when Clarence acts out too much, which is fun to watch. Sometimes she makes mistakes, like when she puts the wrong people in Crayons when they are clearly meant to be in Quills!

BIGGEST FEAR: Blind dates

ONCE I SAW MS. BAKER AT CHUCKLETON'S, WHERE ALL THE FOOD TASTES FUNNY. HA-HA-HA!

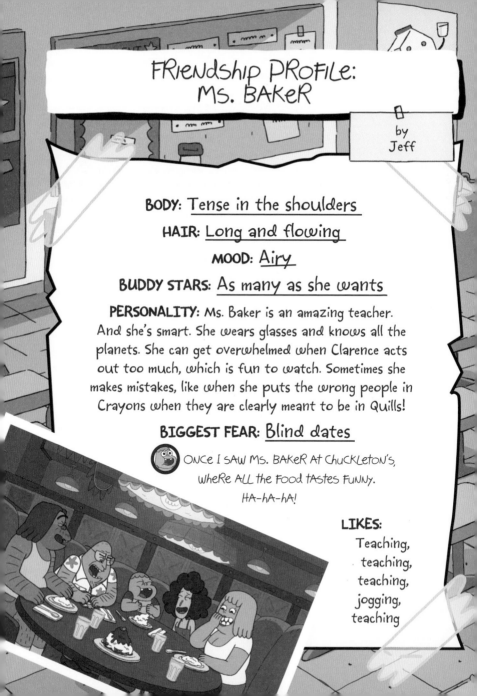

LIKES: Teaching, teaching, teaching, jogging, teaching

WOW! MS. BAKER NEEDS A HOBBY!

DISLIKES: Men in Hawaiian shirts, getting vacuumed by a breadstick, peanut-butter allergies

THAT LAST ONE IS ALL BReehN!

FAVORITE QUOTE: "Don't worry, it's a fun game . . . that you'll be graded on."

FRIENDS: Other teachers, Clarence

SPECIAL TALENTS: Making people use their "listening ears"

MY EARS ARE FOR HOLDING WAX (AND CRICKETS).

FRIENDSHIP PROFILE: MR. REESE

by Clarence

BODY: Side of Beef

HAIR: Some

MOOD: Motivational

BUDDY STARS: *

PERSONALITY: MR. Reese is tough. He used to be a cop, But now he polices the detention room at school. He wants respect from his students and is constantly trying to instill good traits in them, usually by appearing in their dreams with a boat for a head!

BIGGEST FEAR: Getting turned down for a date by Ms. Baker

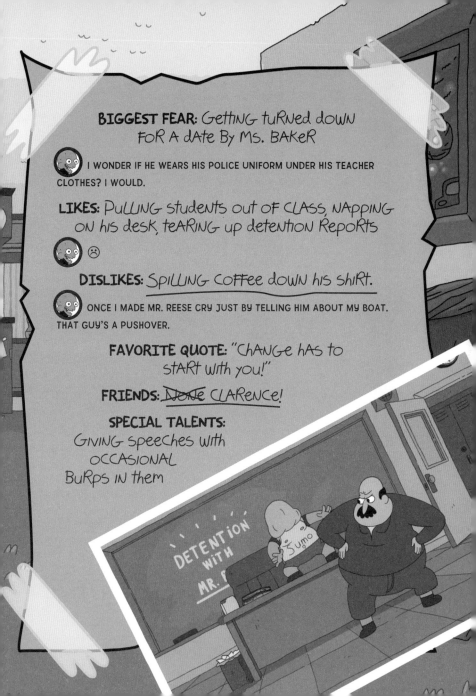 I WONDER IF HE WEARS HIS POLICE UNIFORM UNDER HIS TEACHER CLOTHES? I WOULD.

LIKES: Pulling students out of class, napping on his desk, tearing up detention reports

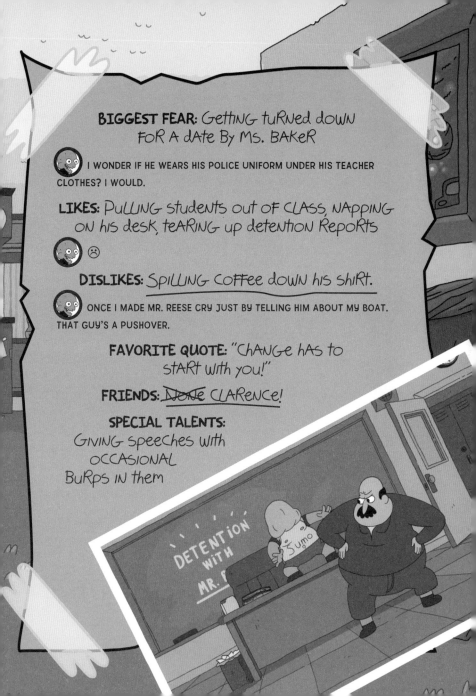

DISLIKES: Spilling coffee down his shirt.

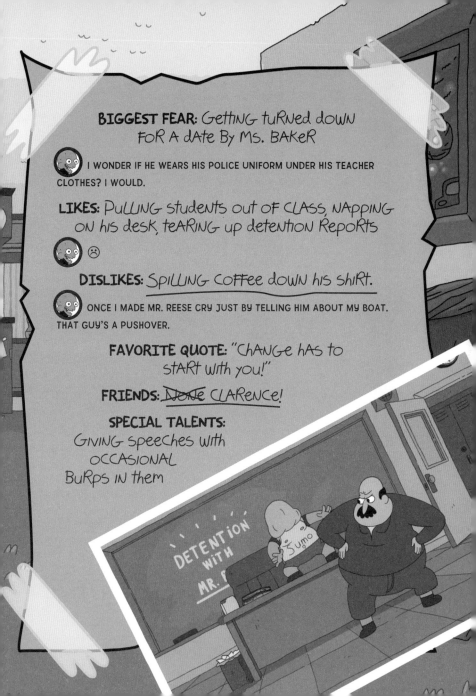 ONCE I MADE MR. REESE CRY JUST BY TELLING HIM ABOUT MY BOAT. THAT GUY'S A PUSHOVER.

FAVORITE QUOTE: "Change has to start with you!"

FRIENDS: ~~Done~~ Clarence!

SPECIAL TALENTS: Giving speeches with occasional burps in them

DETENTION WITH MR.

FRiENDShip PROFiLE: Ms. Shoop

by Sumo

BODY: ROUND (DIAMETER: THREE FEET)

HAIR: BLOND

MOOD: OVER IT

BUDDY STARS: DOESN'T CARE

PERSONALITY: MS. SHOOP IS EXHAUSTED. SHE BARELY HAS ENOUGH ENERGY TO BREATHE, LET ALONE READ A BOOK OUT LOUD!

FUN FACT: MS. BAKER GOT STUCK TEACHING THE QUILLS WHEN MS. SHOOP GOT TO TEACH THE CRAYONS! IS MS. SHOOP LUCKY OR WHAT?

BIGGEST FEAR: ROLLING OVER ON HER CATS IN HER SLEEP

 ONCE I SAW MS. Shoop WALK. THAT'S ALL. IT'S pRetty RARe.

TONYA The TAPIR

LIKES: TAPIRS, FLOWERED DRESSES

DISLIKES: <u>SMILING</u>

FAVORITE QUOTE: "YUM, YUM, YUM. TAPIRS LOVE LEAVES."

FRIENDS: MS. BAKER, JEFF, CLARENCE

 I had a dream that I married Ms. Shoop once. That never would have happened if I were a Quill!

SPECIAL TALENTS: APPEARING IN JEFF'S NIGHTMARES WITH A TAPIR HEAD

 I WONDER Why tEACHeRS ALWAyS AppEAR IN dREAMS WiTH diFFeReNt heAds . . .

FRIENDSHIP PROFILE: ChAd

by Jeff

BODY: <u>Big</u>

HAIR: <u>All over</u>

MOOD: <u>Oblivious</u>

BUDDY STARS: <u>Never heard of them</u>

PERSONALITY: Chad is easygoing, with a tendency to sit on the couch a lot. He really understands Clarence and is more fun than some kids at school. He is kind and won't tell on us if we are about to get into trouble.

 CHAD, YOU DA MAN!

FUTURE JOB: <u>Maybe</u>

SECRET FACT: Chad makes a lot of mistakes. Like when he calls his wallet a "little purse."

OtheR SeCRet FACt: ChAd IS my heRO!

72

BIGGEST FEAR: Forgetting to clean the bathroom. I mean . . . to pick up Clarence at school.

LIKES: Video games, sandals, exposed butt crack, ice cream

DISLIKES: Physical activity, fancy dinners, books, people who talk about their house too much

FAVORITE QUOTE: "You guys getting in trouble in here? I'm hip to it."

FRIENDS: <u>Mary, Jeff, Sumo, Clarence</u>

SPECIAL TALENTS: Falling through ceilings, car accidents, appearing as an airline pilot in Clarence's dreams

I Love ChAd.

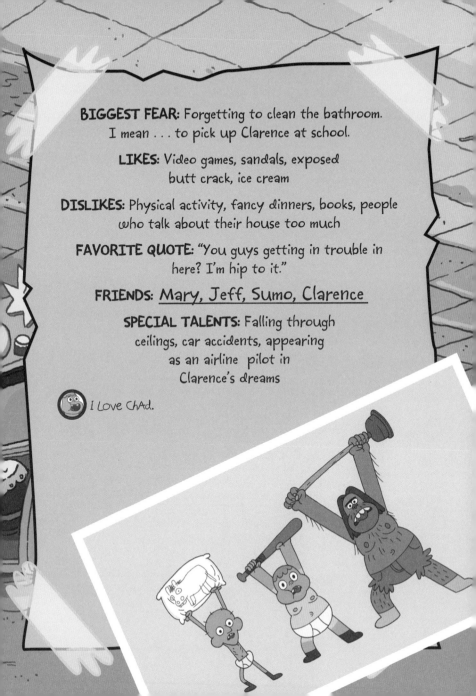

FRIENDSHIP PROFILE: MARY (AKA CLARENCE'S MOM)

by Clarence

BODY: <u>Mom-ish</u>

HAIR: <u>Not NATURAL BLONd</u>

MOOD: <u>LOVING</u>

CLARENCE ~~BUDDY~~ STARS: <u>A MILLION ZILLION</u>

PERSONALITY: Mom is a GReAt mom. She does ALL the RIGht mom thiNGs. She BuYs me FOOd. She huGs me. ANd she doesN't Get thAt mAd WHeN I Get iNto tRouBLe. She teAches me stuFF thAt I Need to KNOw, But isN't mAd iF I doN't Get stRAIGht As Like Jeff.

 Correction: A-plus-plus-plus-plus-pluses!

DREAM VACATION: Trip to the supermarket

BIGGEST FEAR: Running out of the expensive green shampoo

LIKES: Coupons, book clubs, monster-truck jousting

DISLIKES: Clarence's cooking, people who ask for discount haircuts

FAVORITE QUOTE: "Love you, bye. Gotta go. Love you. Bye!"

FRIENDS: Chad, Sumo, Jeff, Clarence

SPECIAL TALENTS: Making egg salad, yelling "Clarence," good advice, leaving us home alone, tucking me in, reading directions, wearing jeans with an elastic waistband, giving allowances, cleaning windows, finding lost toys, sleeping on her side so she doesn't snore like Chad, patience, old-fashioned dance moves, speaking through her nose, being fair, being a grown-up who is also awesome, strong hugs

I LIKE CLARENCE'S MOM BECAUSE SHE'S NICE AND LETS US SLEEP INDOORS!

FRiendship PROfiLE: Kate (AKA NAtuRe KAte)

by Sumo

BODY: <u>EVEN TALLER IN PERSON</u>

HAIR: <u>SMELLS LIKE BRAVERY</u>

MOOD: <u>AMAZING</u>

BUDDY STARS: <u>DOESN'T NEED THEM</u>

PERSONALITY: NATURE KATE IS THE BRAVEST PERSON IN THE WHOLE WIDE STATE PARK SYSTEM. SHE CAN WRANGLE ANY KIND OF ANIMAL AND ISN'T AFRAID OF THE DARK OR NATURE OR ANYTHING. SHE WAS DATING JOSHUA FOR A WHILE, BUT HE CAN'T KEEP UP, SO SHE DUMPED HIM.

BIGGEST FEAR: URBAN SPRAWL

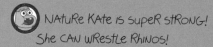

NAtuRe KAte is supeR stRonG! She CAN wRestLe Rhinos!

LIKES: DRIVING HER BRONCO, SAVING PEOPLE WHO ARE FALLING OFF CLIFFS

DISLIKES: GROCERY-STORE CLERKS, PARACHUTES WITHOUT HER FACE ON THEM

FAVORITE QUOTE: "MILK IS NATURE'S MILK."

FRIENDS: JOSHUA (FORMERLY), CLARENCE, SUMO, MOTHER NATURE

SPECIAL TALENTS: HURLING RATTLESNAKES

I gotta agree. She's radder than a rattlesnake. See what I did there?

FRIENDSHIP PROFILE: JOSHUA (AKA GROCERY JOSH)

by
Jeff

BODY: <u>Four rubber bands knotted together</u>

HAIR: <u>Chunk missing due to goat attack</u>

MOOD: <u>Anxious</u>

BUDDY STARS: N/A (attended school prior to start of Buddy Star system)

PERSONALITY: Josh isn't sure what he wants to do with his life, but seems most happy at the supermarket (assistant manager). He's also worked as a waiter at Chuckleton's and as a park ranger, though he's not really good at any of those jobs. Josh does not handle pressure well and freaks out whenever things are going wrong, which is pretty much all the time, thanks to Clarence.

FUN FACT: Josh is always out to impress girls and isn't really good at that, either.

BIGGEST FEAR: <u>Clarence!</u>

Josh tREAts me REAlLy weiRd whenever I see him. I CAN't FiGuRe out why.

LIKES: Ford Pintos, hot tubs, bow ties, dancing in his underwear, falling off cliffs

DISLIKES: Being claw attacked by Sumo, having apple cores thrown at him by Sumo, Sumo kicking the back of his seat, Sumo running away, milk vomit, human chains

AFTER FOUR HOURS IN THE CAR WITH JOSH, YOU'D RUN AWAY, TOO!

FAVORITE QUOTE: "Welcome to Chuckleton's, where everything tastes funny, ha-ha-ha."

FRIENDS: <u>Clarence</u>

JUST FRIENDS: <u>Nature Kate</u>

SPECIAL TALENTS: <u>Delusions</u>

Jeff's Friendship Tips: Final Friendship Thoughts

by Jeff

Well, that's our group project! I hope the advice we gave you will help you build friendships that last a lifetime!

And remember, the key to good friendships is patience, compromise, and being open to new things even if they are the last thing you'd ever want to do.

Who knows, you might learn something!

—Jeff AND CLARENCE AND SUMO

I THINK WE DID A GOOD JOB. EVEN WITH JEFF TRYING TO MESS IT ALL UP!

Yep. Let's cool off by standing on the air conditioner vent until it blows our shirts off!

Oh, and one more tip, before I forget! If you're still having trouble meeting new friends, try giving out some of the CLARENCE DOLLARS I left for you in the last part of this book! WORKS every time!

CLArence
1
1
dollar

CLArence
1
1
dollar

CLArence
1
1
dollar

CLArence
1
1
dollar

CLArence
1
1
dollar

CLArence
1
1
dollar

CLArence
1
1
dollar

CLArence
1
1
dollar

POINT ALEXANDER BRANCH
LAURENTIAN HILLS LIBRARY
34465 HIGHWAY 17, RR #1
DEEP RIVER, ON K0J 1P0